AF228535

INSIDE MLS

COLUMBUS CREW SC

BY THOMAS CAROTHERS

SportsZone

An Imprint of Abdo Publishing
abdobooks.com

abdobooks.com

Published by Abdo Publishing, a division of ABDO, PO Box 398166, Minneapolis, Minnesota 55439. Copyright © 2022 by Abdo Consulting Group, Inc. International copyrights reserved in all countries. No part of this book may be reproduced in any form without written permission from the publisher. SportsZone™ is a trademark and logo of Abdo Publishing.

Printed in the United States of America, North Mankato, Minnesota
052021
092021

Cover Photo: Jason Mowry/Icon Sportswire/AP Images
Interior Photos: Jay LaPrete/AP Images, 5, 7, 18–19, 28; Victor Decolongon/Getty Images Sport/Getty Images, 9; Nick Ut/AP Images, 11; Michael Caulfield/AP Images, 12–13; Rick Stewart/Allsport/Getty Images Sport/Getty Images, 14, 35; Chris Putman/AP Images, 16; Jamie Sabau/Getty Images Sport/Getty Images, 21; Will Shilling/AP Images, 23; Jose L. Marin/Allsport/Getty Images Sport/Getty Images, 25; Gavin Jackson/The Columbus Dispatch/AP Images, 26; Aaron Doster/Cal Sport Media/AP Images, 31; Bill Kostroun/AP Images, 32; Rich Graessle/Icon Sportswire/AP Images, 37; Paul Vernon/AP Images, 39; Jason Mowry/Icon Sportswire, 40–41; Jason Mowry/Icon Sportswire/AP Images, 43

Editor: Patrick Donnelly
Series Designer: Dan Peluso

Library of Congress Control Number: 2019954369

Publisher's Cataloging-in-Publication Data

Names: Carothers, Thomas, author.
Title: Columbus Crew SC / by Thomas Carothers
Description: Minneapolis, Minnesota : Abdo Publishing, 2022 | Series: Inside MLS | Includes online resources and index.
Identifiers: ISBN 9781532192548 (lib. bdg.) | ISBN 9781644945636 (pbk.) | ISBN 9781098210441 (ebook)
Subjects: LCSH: Columbus Crew SC (Soccer team)--Juvenile literature. | Soccer teams--Juvenile literature. | Professional sports franchises--Juvenile literature. | Sports Teams--Juvenile literature.
Classification: DDC 796.334--dc23

TABLE OF CONTENTS

CHAPTER 1

GUNNING FOR
THE CUP

Excitement was high in Columbus when the Crew arrived in 1996. Major League Soccer (MLS) was beginning a new era for the sport in the United States. And for the first time, Ohio's capital city was home to a major professional sports team. More than a decade later, however, that excitement had started to wane.

The Crew had enjoyed some success. Their high-water mark came in 2004 when they won the Supporters' Shield. That trophy goes to the team that finishes the year with the best regular-season record in MLS. But after 12 seasons, they had yet to win the MLS championship.

Mike Clark (3) and his Crew teammates celebrate after winning the 2002 US Open Cup.

CLARK
3

CLOSE, BUT NOT QUITE

Columbus had been fairly successful in its early years. The Crew had qualified for the playoffs in seven of their first nine seasons. In 2002 Columbus won the US Open Cup. That tournament features soccer teams from all levels of competition in the country. The team also advanced to the MLS Eastern Conference finals for the fourth time. Unfortunately, the Crew fell just short of reaching the MLS Cup, just as they had the previous three times.

After missing the playoffs in 2003, Columbus bounced back to go 12–5–13 to win its first Supporters' Shield. But as the top seed in the playoffs, the Crew fell to New England in the conference semifinals.

It was four long years before the Crew qualified for the playoffs again. But they did it in style in 2008. Behind a strong defense led by Chad Marshall, Columbus allowed just 36 goals that season. Only two teams gave up fewer goals. Meanwhile, Venezuelan forward Alejandro Moreno scored nine of the Crew's 50 goals. Only one MLS team scored more that year. What brought it all together, though, was attacking midfielder Guillermo Barros Schelotto. The veteran Argentinian playmaker scored seven goals. No MLS player had more than his 16 assists.

Alejandro Moreno, *right*, fights for the ball against the Chicago Fire in the 2008 Eastern Conference finals.

That led to him winning the league's Most Valuable Player (MVP) award.

Altogether, these players led the Crew to their second Supporters' Shield after posting a 17–7–6 record in the regular season. The Crew then defeated Kansas City and Chicago in the Eastern Conference playoffs. That put them in the MLS championship game at last.

A PAIR OF FIRST-TIMERS

While Columbus had never been to the MLS Cup, the Crew were far from underdogs. They faced the New York Red Bulls, who had made a surprising run to reach the final. New York was another one of the 10 original MLS teams. However, the club had been far less successful than Columbus. Originally named the MetroStars, New York had advanced past the opening round of the MLS playoffs only once. That was in 2000, and that trip ended in the second round.

The Red Bulls weren't expected to reach the title game in 2008. They made the playoffs despite posting a losing record in the regular season. But they shocked two-time defending champion Houston in the conference semifinals on the way to the MLS Cup.

AN MVP SHALL LEAD THEM

It was a sunny day in Los Angeles as the Crew and the Red Bulls took the field. New York had many of the game's best scoring opportunities over the first 30 minutes of play. However, the

Chad Marshall celebrates his go-ahead goal in the second half of the 2008 MLS Cup.

Red Bulls were unable to make good on any of their chances. The game remained scoreless until the 31st minute. That's when the Crew's biggest star, Schelotto, set up the game's first goal.

Schelotto showcased his strong passing skills in the MLS Cup. He claimed the ball along the sideline near midfield. Then he quickly fired a pass to Moreno, who charged toward the New York goal with the ball. Moreno advanced into the box

With the Crew's 2008 MLS Cup win, Sigi Schmid made league history. He became the first coach to win the MLS championship with two different teams. Before coming to Columbus, Schmid coached the Los Angeles Galaxy to the 2002 MLS Cup title. He joined the Crew in 2006 in the middle of three straight sixth-place seasons for the team. Schmid left Columbus to coach Seattle after the 2008 season. In 2019 he became the third person to be inducted into the Crew's Ring of Honor.

and shot the ball past Red Bulls goalkeeper Danny Cepero. The ball found the net just inside the far post, putting Columbus up 1–0.

New York tied the game just six minutes into the second half, but the day belonged to Columbus. Again, it was Schelotto helping his teammates find the goal. Less than two minutes after the Red Bulls scored, the Argentinian lofted a corner kick into the box. Marshall, a player best known for his bruising defense, barged his way past a wall of New York defenders and headed the ball into the net to put Columbus up 2–1.

In the 82nd minute, Schelotto's third assist of the day led to a Frankie Hejduk goal. The 3–1 lead held up, and Columbus had its first MLS Cup trophy. For his hand in all three Columbus goals, Schelotto was named the Man of the Match. Crew captain Hejduk hoisted the gigantic league championship trophy as his teammates celebrated.

Frankie Hejduk kisses the trophy after the Crew beat the New York Red Bulls to win the 2008 MLS Cup.

Thirteen seasons after helping start Major League Soccer, Columbus players and fans were at last able to celebrate a league championship. Through 2019 it remained the only time that the Crew had won the MLS title. But the team has had plenty of other memorable moments along the way.

CHAPTER 2

MLS ORIGINALS

From the start, the Columbus Crew have been one of the more unique teams in MLS. From their location, to their stadium history, to their team badge, the Crew were always a little bit different from the rest.

The Columbus fan base also proved its love of the team by fighting off an attempt to move the Crew to a new city after two decades in its original home. Professional soccer in Columbus was secured for years to come through these efforts.

AN MLS ORIGINAL

The United States won the rights to host the 1994 World Cup. As part of that, officials agreed to create a new professional

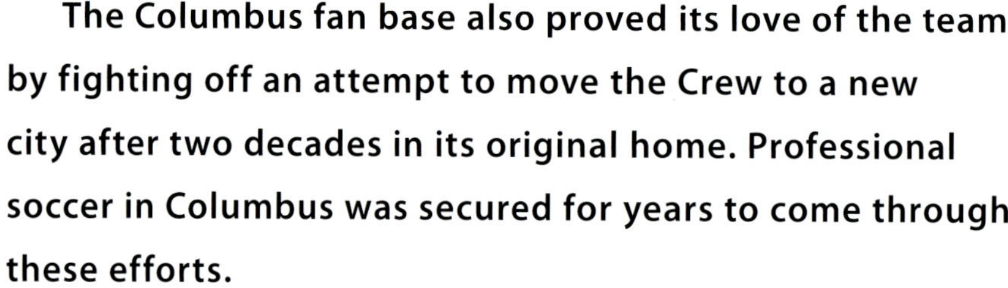

Brian Maisonneuve, right, *of the Crew battles with Dan Calichman of the Los Angeles Galaxy in a 1996 game.*

Brian McBride mingles with young fans after a 1996 game at Ohio Stadium.

soccer league. The United States had been without top-division men's soccer since the North American Soccer League folded in 1984.

The World Cup kicked off on June 17, 1994. Two days earlier, the original 10 MLS teams were announced. Nine of the markets were already home to a major professional team in another sport. However, Columbus was different. Ohio had top-level sports teams in the state's two largest cities, Cleveland and Cincinnati. Columbus had been viewed as a college town, home to Ohio State University. That all changed when MLS came to Ohio's capital city.

Columbus was the smallest of the 10 MLS markets, but the Crew were going to be the only game in town. And its fans were ready for soccer. Building on the momentum generated by the World Cup, the Crew sold more than 9,000 season tickets for their first season.

UNEVEN DEBUT

On April 13, 1996, the Crew played their first game. In front of 25,000 fans, Columbus defeated DC United 4–0 at Ohio Stadium, the home of the Ohio State football team. That first season was a bit of a roller coaster. Coach Timo Liekoski even resigned with 10 games left to play.

However, the Crew went 9–1 over their final 10 games under replacement coach Tom Fitzgerald. Columbus qualified for the playoffs but lost a best-of-three series in the opening round of the Eastern Conference tournament. Still, the team's supporters made an impression. Crew fans were named the best in MLS by *USA Today* after selling 18,950 tickets per game. They also

The Crew opened their new stadium in May 1999.

established a team record by drawing 31,550 fans for the final game of the regular season.

A NEW HOME

Despite averaging nearly 19,000 fans a game, the Crew had a problem. The crowds appeared tiny in the vast expanse of

Ohio Stadium, which seats more than 100,000 fans for college football. It just wasn't a good fit for soccer.

The Crew also knew that Ohio Stadium was set to be remodeled and would soon be unavailable. It did not look good for the team as two attempts to build a new stadium failed. Finally in May 1998, a new stadium was approved.

One year later, Columbus Crew Stadium opened on Ohio's state fairgrounds, just north of downtown. It was the first stadium to be built specifically to host a professional soccer team in the United States. Crew fans bought more than 9,000 season tickets. On May 15, 1999, the stadium opened with Columbus beating New England 2–0 in front of 24,741 fans. That was nearly 2,000 more than the stadium's capacity. The new stadium helped Columbus average 17,696 fans, which was the best in the league that season.

FILLING THE TROPHY CASE

Columbus's new stadium helped put the city on the American soccer map. The Crew hosted the MLS All-Star Game in 2000. The US men's national team also played a handful of matches there in 2000. In 2001 the stadium hosted the MLS Cup. This was back when the final was played at a neutral site.

Brian McBride, *left*, and Brian Dunseth cheer as they receive the US Open Cup trophy in 2002.

While Columbus had become a destination for top-level soccer, the team had yet to arrive at the top level itself. That all changed in 2002 when the Crew won the US Open Cup. The tournament dates back to 1913, making it the oldest soccer tournament in the country. All clubs that are sanctioned

by the US Soccer Federation are eligible to compete in the knockout competition.

Columbus hosted the final against the LA Galaxy, who had just won the MLS Cup four days earlier. Crew midfielder Freddy Garcia scored the game's lone goal as Columbus earned the

Lamar Hunt made his name as a visionary owner and executive in American football. He also left quite the mark in soccer. When MLS was founded, it needed owners willing to take a risk. Hunt was one of them, signing up to own both the Crew and Kansas City Wizards (now Sporting KC). He later bought the MLS team in his hometown of Dallas, too. Hunt helped secure the future of soccer in Columbus when he financed the construction of the Crew's home stadium. He died in 2006, and four years later a statue saluting Hunt was unveiled at Crew Stadium. His family sold the team in 2013.

first trophy in team history in a 1–0 win.

INTERNATIONAL DEBUT

By winning the US Open Cup, the Crew qualified for the 2003 Concacaf Champions' Cup tournament. The Champions' Cup, now known as the Concacaf Champions League, is played every year. It features the top club teams from North America, Central America, and the Caribbean.

Columbus won its first-round matchup of the 16-team tournament against Árabe Unido of Panama. However, the Crew fell to Mexico's Monarcas Morelia in the quarterfinals to end their international run.

The Crew went on to qualify for the Concacaf Champions League in 2009 and 2010. Both times they reached the quarterfinals again before bowing out.

Family members pose with the statue of Lamar Hunt after its unveiling outside Columbus Crew Stadium in 2010.

CHAPTER 3

STANDOUT PLAYERS

As one of the original MLS teams, the Crew have seen a number of top players don their black and yellow uniforms over the years. Whether they were stars who made their names in foreign leagues or homegrown players who established themselves in Columbus, each has put his own stamp on the history of professional soccer in Ohio's capital city.

HOMEGROWN HEROES

One of the first steps for the original MLS teams was building a roster. One way they did that was through the MLS draft. Columbus, picking first, selected forward Brian McBride. He would go down as the first of a number of standout American players to shine in a Crew uniform.

US national team star Brian McBride spent eight seasons with the Crew before taking his talents to Fulham in England's Premier League.

McBride had grown up in the Chicago area and then starred at St. Louis University. Prior to the start of MLS, he played a season for Wolfsburg in Germany's second division. He was still just 23 years old when the Crew kicked off. Yet McBride quickly showed signs of the elite player he was to become.

He scored 17 goals in 28 league games during his first season in Columbus. Despite missing parts of two seasons while playing on loan in England, McBride scored 62 goals with 45 assists during his eight years with the Crew. He held the team's all-time goal-scoring record until 2011. McBride also became a key player for the US national team, taking part in three World Cups.

McBride retired in 2010. In 2014 he was inducted into the National Soccer Hall of Fame, in part for his efforts as a member of the Crew. He also was the first former Crew member to be inducted into the team's Circle of Honor.

Goalkeeper Brad Friedel joined McBride in Columbus with 10 games left in the 1996 season. It was no coincidence that the team won nine of its final 10 games and made the playoffs. An Ohio native, Friedel played one more season with the Crew in 1997 before his contract was sold to Liverpool in the English Premier League. That began an 18-year run in England for

Brad Friedel, who played goalkeeper for the United States in the 2002 World Cup, spent parts of two seasons with Columbus.

Frankie Hejduk, *right*, anchored the Crew's back line for eight seasons.

Friedel, who also had a successful career with the US national team. Friedel won 22 matches and posted 11 shutouts in 38 appearances for Columbus.

Like Friedel, Frankie Hejduk played his college soccer at the University of California, Los Angeles (UCLA). The two Bruins both have a special place in the hearts of Crew fans. Columbus was Hejduk's second MLS stop. He began his career with the

Tampa Bay Mutiny. That led to him playing a little more than four seasons in Germany. Upon returning home to the United States, he immediately found a home with the Columbus defense. Hejduk played in 147 games for the team from 2003 to 2010.

Known for his long hair and easygoing vibe, Hejduk quickly became a fan favorite. His time with the Crew defense also came during some of the most successful years for the team. He captained the 2008 squad that won Columbus's first MLS Cup championship. The Crew also won the MLS Supporters' Shield three times (2004, 2008, 2009) with Hejduk in defense.

After his retirement in 2012, Hejduk joined the Crew front office as a team ambassador. In 2014 he became the second player inducted into the Crew's Circle of Honor.

POLISH RIFLE

Robert Warzycha played for the Crew during their inaugural season in 1996. He stayed in Columbus for the next 18 years. A right winger by trade, Warzycha played seven seasons with the Crew before retiring as the team's all-time leader with 61 assists. He became known as "the Polish Rifle" to Crew fans in part for his powerful free kicks.

After injuries forced him from the pitch, he remained on the sideline as a member of the Crew coaching staff in 2003. He became the team's coach in 2009, winning one Supporters' Shield, before he was let go in 2013. His son, Konrad Warzycha, also played one season in Columbus.

Guillermo Barros Schelotto, *left*, won the MLS MVP Award in 2008.

While Hejduk scored the final goal of the Crew's MLS Cup victory in 2008, it was fellow California native and defender Chad Marshall who gave them a 2–1 lead. Marshall's thundering strike is an iconic moment in club history, but he was far from a one-trick pony. The second pick of the 2004 MLS SuperDraft played 10 years in Columbus. During that time he established himself as one of the league's toughest defenders. In fact, he was named MLS Defender of the Year in 2008 and 2009, before winning it a third time after leaving Columbus. In total, Marshall set club records with 250 games started and 22,220 minutes played. Like his fellow defender Hejduk, Marshall won three Supporters' Shields and an MLS Cup.

GOING GLOBAL

Throughout MLS history, international players have starred alongside their American counterparts. Few in league history have had quite the impact as Guillermo Barros Schelotto.

Schelotto arrived in Columbus in 2007 after a long and successful career with Boca Juniors in his native Argentina. Though he was already in his mid-30s, Schelotto went on to become the greatest player during the most successful run in Crew history. Schelotto was a forward with a talent for making his teammates better. He posted 33 goals and 41 assists over 102 games with Columbus from 2007 to 2010.

The high point of Schelotto's Crew career was in 2008. He was named the league's MVP while leading his team to the best regular-season record. With Schelotto leading the attack, Columbus won the Supporters' Shield and its first MLS Cup.

After assisting on all three goals of the Crew's 3–1 win over the New York Red Bulls, Schelotto capped off 2008 by being named MLS Cup MVP.

Schelotto returned to his native Argentina in 2011 to close out his playing career, though he came back to coach the Los Angeles Galaxy in 2019. In 2012 the Crew went back to Argentina to find their next big playmaker. Federico Higuaín joined Columbus late in 2012 and scored five goals with seven assists in just 13 games. In 2013 the attacking midfielder picked up right where he left off by scoring on opening day. That was part of back-to-back 11-goal seasons for Higuaín. In 2015 he helped the Crew return to the MLS Cup, where they lost to Portland.

During eight seasons with Columbus, Higuaín scored 55 goals with 63 assists. He is the only player in Crew history to score 50 goals with 50 assists. Through 2020 just 21 players in MLS history have accomplished the feat.

CARIBBEAN CONNECTION

While Argentina has been good to Columbus, so has the Caribbean. Two of the Crew's best all-time forwards have come from the tiny islands in the form of Jeff Cunningham and Stern John. Both began their time in Columbus in 1998.

Federico Higuaín scores on a penalty kick in a 2013 match.

John played just two seasons with the Crew, but they were memorable ones. The native of Trinidad and Tobago burst on the scene in 1998 with an MLS-best 26 goals and 57 points. The next season he added 18 more goals before he was sold

Jeff Cunningham, *left*, is the top scorer in Crew history.

to Nottingham Forest in England. Despite playing just two seasons in Columbus, 20 years later he remained fourth all-time on the club's career scoring list with 44 goals.

Cunningham's career with the Crew lasted a bit longer. After forming a strong partnership with John in 1998 and 1999, Cunningham remained in Columbus through 2004. The Jamaican holds the team's all-time goal-scoring record with 64.

In 2011 Cunningham returned to Columbus for his final MLS season. He scored two goals in his last campaign to become the team's all-time leading scorer. He retired in 2012 with 135 career goals, an MLS record later broken by Landon Donovan.

ZARDES IN THE ZONE

When the Crew traded for Gyasi Zardes in 2018, nobody knew which player they would get. Zardes scored 16 goals for the LA Galaxy in 2014 as the club won the MLS Cup. But by 2017, injuries limited Zardes to just two goals. The California native and US national team standout found a new home with the Crew, leading the team in scoring in each of his first three seasons. His 44 league goals with the Crew placed him in the top five in club history.

CHAPTER 4

BIG
MOMENTS

May 10, 1994, was one of the biggest days in Columbus Crew history. On that day, the city of Columbus met the league's demand for 10,000 season-ticket deposits. Then the team's application was submitted to MLS for approval.

The team became known as the Crew via a fan contest. But another name has been lost to history. When the Columbus ownership group first sent the team's application to MLS for approval, it used the name "Eclipse." While the name fit at first—Columbus eclipsed 10,000 season-ticket deposits on the day of an actual solar eclipse—it did not stick.

Among the original 10 MLS markets, Columbus was the only one to hit the 10,000-deposit mark. Thus, the league

Columbus soccer fans young and old supported the Crew from the start.

rewarded the fans by recognizing the Crew as the first league franchise when MLS announced its lineup on June 15, 1994.

Doug Logan, the first commissioner in MLS history, began to announce which cities would host teams. The first logo to appear behind him was that of the new Columbus Crew. It was different from the other team logos in that it featured people. The original logo showed three stern-faced men in hard hats. It was meant to suggest a "work-hard, show-me-don't-tell-me attitude." It also pointed to the importance of teamwork. The logo remained until 2014, when the Crew added "SC" for "Soccer Club" to the end of its name. Then it adopted a more traditional-looking crest.

ANOTHER RUN TO THE CUP

The Crew came into the 2015 season with some momentum. Under first-year coach Gregg Berhalter, the team had snapped a two-year playoff drought in 2014. With midfielders Federico Higuaín, Wil Trapp, and Justin Meram leading the way, the Crew entered 2015 with championship aspirations.

Behind veteran forward Kei Kamara, who tied for the league lead with 22 goals, Columbus had one of the league's most dangerous offenses. The team also played with an

Dynamic goal scorer Kei Kamara led the Crew on a deep playoff run in 2015.

attractive style. And after going 15–11–8, Columbus entered the playoffs as the No. 2 seed in the Eastern Conference.

Twice, the Crew faced close calls. After losing 2–1 to the Montreal Impact in the playoff opener, the Crew needed a two-goal win at home in the return leg. Through 76 minutes of play, however, the game was tied 1–1. Then Ethan Finlay scored a goal that tied the aggregate score 3–3. In extra time, Kamara scored his second goal of the game to send the Crew on.

The conference finals were the opposite. After beating the New York Red Bulls 2–0 at home, the Crew went down 1–0 in the waning minutes of the second game. A potentially tying shot for New York went off the post. Columbus was able to hold on and win the series.

That sent the Crew to their second MLS Cup and first since 2008. This time they hosted the championship game on their home field. However, the Portland Timbers scored on a misplayed ball just 27 seconds into the game. Then the Timbers scored again in the seventh minute. Kamara got the Crew back into the game with a hard shot in the 18th minute. It proved to be not quite enough, however, as the Timbers prevailed in a gritty 2–1 win.

Defender Michael Parkhurst, *left*, and the Crew came up just short against Portland in the 2015 MLS Cup.

AN ERA OF CHANGE

On July 30, 2013, the Hunt Sports Group announced some big news. The group, which still owned the Crew and was run by Hunt's son Clark, said that it was selling the team to California

"Save The Crew" became the fans' rallying cry when a new owner threatened to move the team.

businessman Anthony Precourt. Precourt brought about a number of changes, including new uniforms, adding the "SC" to the Crew name, and making improvements to Crew Stadium.

But behind the scenes, Precourt began to talk to the city of Austin, Texas, about the possibility of moving the team there. Columbus fans responded with a "Save The Crew" campaign in October 2017. Ohio politicians pitched in to try to save the team as well. Together, they saved the Crew.

On October 12, 2018, it was announced that a group
based in Columbus was going to buy the team and keep it in
Columbus. The group was headed by Crew team doctor Pete
Edwards and Jimmy Haslam, owner of the Cleveland Browns.
The day is now known as "Save The Crew Day" in Columbus.

A NEW BEGINNING

On the field, the club struggled. Despite the presence of
high-scoring forward Gyasi Zardes, Columbus finished 10th in

the Eastern Conference in 2019. The one bright spot came on October 11, when the club cemented its future in Columbus by breaking ground on a new stadium.

Things looked brighter for the Crew in 2020. That offseason they traded for Darlington Nagbe, who had been one of MLS' most effective midfielders. The new owners also invested in the club by signing Argentinian midfielder Lucas Zelarayan from the Mexican league. Team captain Jonathan Mensah, meanwhile, was back to anchor a strong defense.

Despite a season that was interrupted for months by the COVID-19 pandemic, Columbus thrived. The club finished third in the East.

After giving up two goals in the first round of the playoffs, the Crew didn't allow a single goal the rest of the way. That included the MLS Cup at home in Columbus. Playing the mighty Seattle Sounders, Zelarayan opened the scoring with

The Crew broke ground on a new stadium in October 2019.

a 25th-minute goal on the volley. Zelarayan, who was named
MLS Newcomer of the Year, added a goal in the 82nd minute in
a 3–0 rout.

It was the biggest margin of victory in MLS Cup history.
Crew fans had a championship team that was theirs for good.
For a team with an important place in MLS history, the Crew
were once again plotting a bold course for the future.

TIMELINE

1994	1996	1999	2002	2003
The Crew are announced as one of 10 original MLS teams on June 15.	Columbus defeats DC United 4–0 on April 13 in its first MLS game.	Crew Stadium opens on May 15 with a 2–0 win over New England.	The Crew win the US Open Cup, the team's first trophy, with a 1–0 defeat of the LA Galaxy on October 24.	Columbus competes in its first Concacaf Champions League game on March 16

2008	2013	2015	2018	2020
The Crew defeat the New York Red Bulls 3–1 on November 23 to win their first MLS Cup.	Hunt Sports Group announces the sale of the Crew to Anthony Precourt on July 30.	The Crew reach the MLS Cup for the second time, but they fall to Portland 2–1 on December 6.	Precourt officially sells the Crew to a group headed by Pete Edwards and Jimmy and Dee Haslam on December 28.	Columbus beats Seattle 3-0 to win the second MLS Cup in team history

TEAM FACTS

FIRST SEASON

1996

STADIUMS

Ohio Stadium (1996–98)
Columbus Crew Stadium (1999–2021)
New Columbus Crew Stadium (2021–)

MLS CUP TITLES

2008, 2020

US OPEN CUP TITLES

2002

SUPPORTERS' SHIELDS

2004, 2008, 2009

KEY PLAYERS

Jeff Cunningham (1998–2004, 2011)
Frankie Hejduk (2003–10)
Federico Higuaín (2012–19)
Stern John (1998–99)
Chad Marshall (2004–13)
Brian McBride (1996–2003)
Jonathan Mensah (2017–)
Guillermo Barros Schelotto (2007–10)
Gyasi Zardes (2018–)

KEY COACHES

Greg Andrulis (2001–05)
Gregg Berhalter (2014–18)
Sigi Schmid (2006–08)
Robert Warzycha (2008–13)

MLS MOST VALUABLE PLAYER

Guillermo Barros Schelotto (2008)

MLS DEFENDER OF THE YEAR

Robin Fraser (2004)
Chad Marshall (2008, 2009)

MLS NEWCOMER OF THE YEAR

Federico Higuaín (2012)
Lucas Zelarayan (2020)

**MLS GOALKEEPER OF
THE YEAR**

Brad Friedel (1997)
Zack Steffen (2018)

**MLS HUMANITARIAN OF
THE YEAR**

Kei Kamara (2015)

MLS ROOKIE OF THE YEAR

Kyle Martino (2002)

**MLS COMEBACK PLAYER OF
THE YEAR**

Gyasi Zardes (2018)

MLS COACH OF THE YEAR

Greg Andrulis (2004)
Sigi Schmid (2008)

GLOSSARY

aggregate
The combined score of both games in a two-game series.

ambassador
A representative or messenger.

assist
A pass that leads directly to a goal.

franchise
A sports organization, including the top-level team and all minor league affiliates.

free kick
An unguarded kick awarded to a team after an opponent's foul.

inaugural
Marking the beginning of an institution, activity, or period of office.

knockout
A kind of competition in which one loss eliminates a team.

loan
An agreement that allows a player to play for another team for a single season or less.

midfielder
A player who stays mostly in the middle third of the field and links the defenders with the forwards.

underdog
The person or team that is not expected to win.

winger
A player who plays in a wide position on the field, taking part both in attack and defense.

MORE **INFORMATION**

BOOKS

Kortemeier, Todd. *Total Soccer*. Minneapolis, MN: Abdo Publishing, 2017.

Marthaler, Jon. *Ultimate Soccer Road Trip*. Minneapolis, MN: Abdo Publishing, 2019.

Trusdell, Brian. *Soccer Record Breakers*. Minneapolis, MN: Abdo Publishing, 2016.

ONLINE RESOURCES

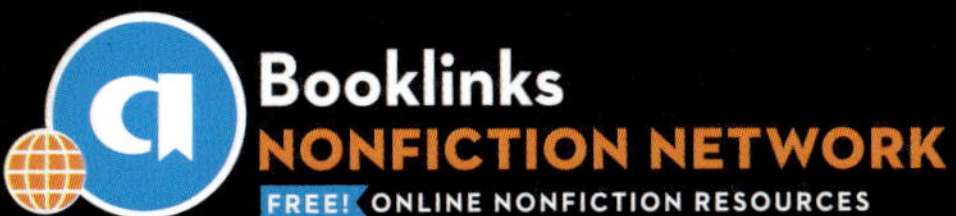

To learn more about Columbus Crew SC, please visit **abdobooklinks.com** or scan this QR code. These links are routinely monitored and updated to provide the most current information available.

INDEX

ABOUT THE AUTHOR

Thomas Carothers has been a sportswriter for nearly 20 years in the Minneapolis/St. Paul, Minnesota, area. He has worked for a number of print and online publications, mostly focusing on prep sports coverage. He lives in Minneapolis with his wife and a houseful of dogs.